JELLY
J FISH
PRESS

Catching Snow

STELLA QUINN

The moral right of the author has been asserted.
No part of this book may be reproduced, stored in a retrieval system,
or transmitted by any means, electronic, mechanical, by photocopier
or otherwise, without the prior written consent of the author.

This is a work of fiction. While the locations in this book are a
mixture of real and imagined, the characters are totally fictitious. Any
resemblance to actual people living or dead is entirely coincidental.

"Good things of day begin to droop and drowse;
while night's black agents to their preys do rouse."

William Shakespeare
Macbeth

CATCHING SNOW

The first drops of snow fell as Lisa stood by the faded red door of historic Dunstone Station. She cupped her hands, catching the white crystals only to see them dissolve into the crimson wool of her gloves. Like catching tears, she thought. Behind her, the hiss and squeal of iron on steel marked the departure of the train that had raced her up into the mountains northwest of Sacramento.

Usually, stepping from the station into the clear mountain air made her feel like she was coming home. But not today. Not this trip. Grief had cloaked her the way snow would soon cloak the ground. If only she hadn't been so far away.

She twisted her watch around on her wrist. A few minutes after three, but the afternoon had closed in. Street lamps sent a golden glow over the gracious old buildings of Dunstone. Fairy lights and baubles in windows, the trill of laughter and carols ... such festive noises; how she envied those happy people. Turning her back on them, she focused on the cab she could see idling at the curb by the Café Carlotta.

Steam puffed from its exhaust into the snow-heavy air, and

a dusting of white covered its bonnet. Pulling her jacket more firmly around her, Lisa slung her well-worn backpack over her shoulder and set off. Lingering in the cold on a freezing sidewalk in a remote mountain town wasn't going to make her feel better. Nothing was, not until she made it to Aggie's house. Maybe then she'd be able to say goodbye.

'Where to, love?'

The cabbie wasn't the usual old grizzle-guts, Pete, who hated leaving the well-groomed blacktop roads of Dunstone.

'River's End Road – the top end.'

'Jump in, before you freeze. I've not been out that way yet, can you direct me?'

What, no complaining about the pot holes? The damage the loose gravel would do to his cab's canary yellow paintwork? Last visit she would have grinned. She kicked the loose snow from her boots and bundled herself into the backseat of the cab. 'I can direct you.'

The interior of the car felt like a sauna after the cold of the street, and she shrugged out of her gloves and beanie, tucking them into the pockets of her jacket. Her fingers scuffed over the thick wad of letters she'd stuffed in there – when? Was it just this morning? She'd lost her sense of time somewhere in the fog of jetlag and grief.

What a day. What a crushing, horrid, bust of a day.

She'd been so chuffed about returning to the States for Christmas after a six month absence. Her backpack was stuffed with research notes and photos, her head filled with stories and hope, all of which she'd been planning to share with Aggie. But when she'd stopped in at the head office in Rarotonga on her way through from Aitutaki to the airport, at the start of her twenty-six-hour slog from the Cook Islands to San Francisco, all those plans had come to a screaming, juddering halt.

She didn't need to pull the envelopes out to read them. The black handwriting was burned in her memory, postmarked Dunstone, addressed to *Lisa Wu, Research Scientist, c/- Ocean Angels, Rarotonga, Cook Islands*. If only she'd known! If only she'd been home. But she hadn't. She'd been out on an atoll with no access to the internet, busy on the giant clam breeding project she ran. She'd barely had running water, let alone the ability to communicate with the person who meant more to her than the world. She pressed her cold hand to her colder face. She'd never forgive herself for not being here when she was needed. Never.

The old-fashioned loops of Aggie's writing swirled through her mind.

Darling Lisa, I do so hope your project is going well, and the baby clams are putting on weight. I've been a little out of sorts lately, nothing to worry about ...'

Darling Lisa, it might be a week or two until I write again, the doctors are insisting I go into hospital for a few days, just until my new blood pressure medication sorts itself out ...'

Darling Lisa, I can't tell you how much it cheers me to think of my letters flying over blue seas and coral and whales and fish, on their way to you in your island research camp, from me in this dreary hospital room. If I could squeeze myself into the envelope, I would do it in an instant, my girl.

Do you remember those flowers we used to press into the pages of my books when you were small? I'd like to preserve myself the same way now, and come and visit you and smell the salt air.

Now, I don't want you to do anything silly when you read this, like come home, because that is NOT what I want. I want you there, on

9

Aitutaki, living your dreams, not wasting my time and cluttering up the end of my bed with any nonsensical weeping.

However, I should tell you, the doctors have started muttering and tutting when they read my bloodwork results, and something is afoot, which has reminded me of something that I should let you know.

I redid my will years ago, after your mother passed away, but I never got around to sending it to that dollar-guzzling lawyer in his fancy-pants office in town. It's in a book, pressed between two of my favorite pages. Now if only I could remember which book. Anne of Green Gables, *maybe? Or perhaps the first edition of* Heidi.

You'll find it, if you need to. After all, you are my only living relative now …'

And then the final one. The letter that started in Aggie's dear scrawl, but ended in the neat cursive of a kind stranger.

'…Dear Lisa. Our patient, Agatha Wendall, passed away this morning after a difficult few days. She was quite insistent last night that her letter to you be posted, so I am fulfilling her wish.

May I offer you my condolences on the loss of your friend.

Yours faithfully, Selma Rajnathapuri, RN.'

A jolt of wheels through rough road brought Lisa out of herself, and she looked up, surprised to see they had reached the upper twists and turns of River's End Road already.

'Much further, love?' said the cabbie, peering forward into gloom. Valley oak trees formed a dark arbor over the road ahead, and the snowfall had thickened, flurries of white drifting through the branches to carpet the gravel below.

'There's a turn just ahead,' she said. 'With a red signpost. Maybe a hundred yards further up.'

The taxi rolled forward and she spied the red sign. Beyond,

down a lane that wound through a field of lavender, she could see the corner of a house. Her house, now. Aggie's riverstone and cedar mountain cabin – the place in her life that held her happiest memories.

She tried to speak but words were hard to find. Her throat was tight with raw emotion. She hadn't realized it would be so hard to return here, where Aggie wasn't.

She fumbled at the handle. 'I'll walk from here.'

'You sure? I can drive up there, no problem. It's getting dark, young lady, and poor weather's on its way in, according to the radio.'

She had to be alone. She needed to be alone, just her, with the mountain as her witness, while she walked into the Aggie-shaped hole that was her future. 'No, it's fine, but thanks. I've got someone waiting for me.'

A lie, but a little one. All that was waiting for her at the end of the drive was her memories.

She fumbled in her wallet for money, and handed the rumpled notes through the gap between the front seats. 'Keep the change,' she said.

The cabbie turned his car in a narrow sweep of headlights and crunching tires, and she waited until the roar of his engine had died away before shouldering her pack.

Finally, she was home.

***

Ryan Mulligan checked the reception bars on the screen of his phone. No bars. He tapped a long finger on the internet app. No service, either. He grinned. Finally, *finally*, he'd be able to get some peace.

He tucked his phone into his back pocket, adjusted the

holster he wore around his shoulder, and assessed the mounting pile of firewood he'd spent the last hour cutting. A few more, he thought. A storm was galloping in over Mount Shasta, if he was reading that black cloud right. And he planned on riding it out by the fire in his newly acquired mountain cabin.

Alone. Gloriously alone. Just him, the fire, a beer or two – and not a goddamn reporter or police uniform in sight. Even the stray dog that had turned up at the cabin a time or two, looking for food and affection, had disappeared.

He swung the axe down into the log on the block, grunting with satisfaction as it cleaved along the grain. He was beginning to get the hang of this mountain life. Maybe he'd snare a rabbit later – toss it in a hotpot with some wild greens. He snorted. As if. A steak on the grill and a spud in the microwave was about the limit of his culinary skills.

But that could change. God knows, something needed to. He couldn't keep going the way he had been, he'd be a nutcase on stress leave if he didn't learn to take a break from the job.

Chucking the last of the split logs onto the woodpile, he gathered up the basket of kindling he'd collected earlier and headed over to the cabin's back porch. He took a glance around before he went in. From habit, mostly. A cop who spent his on-duty hours hunting down the scum of the earth could never relax, not really.

He shook his head. No binoculars glinted back at him from the thickly wooded tree line. No victims semaphored morse code from the white-tipped mountain ridges rearing into the heavy sky.

He *could* relax, damn it. Wasn't that what he was doing out here in the wilderness? He could get the hell off the high alert he'd been living on for the past few months as he'd pursued

Sacramento's worst serial killer in thirty years. He sucked in a breath of the frigid air, let it out slowly. Maybe in a week or two he'd even stop feeling he had to strap his police-issue colt on in the morning when he rolled out of bed.

No-one at work knew he was here, not even his boss. Sure as hell not the media who'd been trying to turn him into a celebrity ever since he'd made the arrest. *Hero Cop Takes Down The Strangler.* He snorted. They'd driven him half mad with their headlines and pestering and dumbass questions. He was no hero, he'd just been doing his job.

Take three weeks, the Chief of the Sacramento Police had said. Three weeks to let the media storm die down, take a break, then come back ready to start work on a new case. It had been on day one of his vacation that he'd seen the ad for the cabin.

Difficult to access in winter, the description had read. Perfect. *No immediate neighbors* – even better. *Fully furnished. Suit home renovator.* Okay, the furniture was a plus. And he knew what a hammer was, he just hadn't had much cause to use one. He was a city slicker, born and bred. In his experience, home renovations came in a flat pack on a delivery truck.

It was the last line that was the clincher: *available for immediate occupancy.* He'd phoned the number, spoken to some jackass who sounded like his windpipe was permanently constricted by a suit and tie, paid his deposit and picked up the keys that afternoon in Dunstone.

Sure, the legals'd take a few weeks to clear, something to do with the deceased estate having no beneficiaries – but he got to live in the cabin while it cleared. A trunk full of groceries later, and here he was.

He rested his hand on the ornate handle sticking out of the solid back door, and winced as the frozen metal bit into his fingers. Note to self – wear gloves next time he went outside. The temperature was in freefall out here in the yard. He turned the handle, and cranked the door open wide to let himself and his kindling into the open plan ground floor of the cabin. A sound had him jerking to attention like a spark of fat on a fire.

'What the—'

It took a heartbeat to assess the front door – ajar when he'd had it shut and locked. And the entry foyer – cluttered with a battered knapsack when he'd left it bare and freshly swept. But a heartbeat was all it took to have his gun in his hand and every cop sense he'd honed in fifteen years on the force screaming *intruder*.

Okay, the knapsack was an odd touch. A lost mountain hiker, looking for shelter from the snow storm that was building, perhaps? His adrenalin eased off a touch, but the pressure of his fingers on his gun didn't. He'd know soon enough – the scrape of boots on the flagged step outside the front door carried clearly through the room.

The sun had disappeared behind mountain or cloud, or both, in the time he'd spent messing about outdoors. The cabin was dim inside, and cold. The fire had sputtered out, and he'd not found the thermostat for the boiler before he'd headed outside to wear himself out with yard work.

But then a woman stepped through the front door and his cop thoughts scrambled. Man thoughts came rushing in, filling the vacuum that had been created by the rapid exit of his common sense and intuition. Hot, urgent, pulse-hammering man thoughts.

Brown hair shot with gold framed the delicate face, falling down in impossibly long waves past her shoulders, ending somewhere in the curve between rib and hip. A woolen hat the color of a fire engine was pulled over her head, matching the red gloves she wore.

She hadn't seen him yet in the dark recess of the cabin. He lowered his gun, pointing it at the floor. She had no weapon, not unless she'd tucked it into the battered anorak she wore, or somewhere on that long, long, length of leg that disappeared into fur trimmed boots that looked like they'd traveled the length and breadth of North California.

An intruder, but a heart-stoppingly hot one. And she looked about as violent as a fancy teacup.

She slid a red gloved hand up the inside of the front door and snicked it shut, throwing the cabin into darkness for a millisecond, but an instant later the overhead lights flickered on as she flipped the switch.

He stepped forward into the light.

***

Lisa flipped the switch, hoping the electricity was still connected. Heaven only knew how overdue Aggie's utility bills were – it had been a month since Aggie died, and she'd been in the hospital before that. Her mental list of things to do was getting longer by the second. But getting the fire going was definitely job number one, it was freezing in h—

Her inner list-making froze. Her gaze zip-locked to the stranger standing in Aggie's old-fashioned kitchen. And was that—? Holy crap, it was. She let out a shrill squeak and pressed her back up against the solid wood of the door behind her. Why, oh why, was there a man with a gun staring her down across the narrow width of Aggie's mountain cabin?

She felt like she'd stumbled into a scene from an old western – only, there was no honkytonk piano music cheering the mood, and she sure wasn't feeling entertained.

'Who the hell are you?' she said into the silence. If she was about to be gunned down she may as well know the name of the guy about to do the gunning.

The man took a step forward further into the light, and she scrabbled her gloved hand behind her, feeling for the handle. Should she run? But where to? Her brain started assimilating facts: the box of groceries and pile of newspapers on the table, the basket of kindling he'd dropped to the floor ... and his face. He looked serious. Like a college jock who'd grown up and learned a bunch of hard lessons that had cut the fun out of life. Or a movie star who'd made the switch from romcom to drama.

She shivered. Whoever this man was, he looked tough. Intimidating, with close-cropped hair, and two-day stubble, and eyes that looked like they could stare down the devil. She thought longingly of the snug taxi, whooshing its way over snow-lined roads back to town. Why hadn't she accepted the driver's offer to accompany her to the house?

The man seemed to reach a decision, because he tucked the gun into the dark leather of some sort of holster, and shrugged out of the heavy jacket he was wearing. A flurry of snow dislodged itself all over Aggie's kitchen floor.

'My name's Ryan. I live here. Who are you? And I'd be interested to know why you have a key to my house.'

His house? The shock of his statement arrested the panic that had been clawing at her nerves since the sight of the man and his gun. Her brain, seasoned by years of scientific study to gather facts and produce logical conclusions, scrambled like eggs in a skillet as she watched him remove his jacket. What had he said?

She tried to cling on to the words, but fear and fatigue had eroded her ability to process. Her eyes fixed on the gun holster strapped across his chest, skittered across the close-fitting navy sweater he wore. Her thoughts fragmented into the bare essentials: Ryan, live here, gun strapped to muscle. Her over-tired brain decided it was easier to answer his question than understand the cues.

'I'm Lisa Wu. This is my grandmother's cabin. At least,' her breath hitched, 'it was. Aggie left it to me when she died.' She felt stronger saying the words, strong enough to counter his claim, gun or no gun. 'So Ryan, I'd be interested to know why you have a key to *my* house.'

The man frowned. 'That can't be right – I've just bought it.'

'What? From whom?'

'A lawyer in Dunstone. Gave me the keys two days ago when I signed the contract.'

'Oh no, no.' Tears welled up and she dashed them away. Crying wouldn't solve anything.

'Hey, it's okay. Let's ju—'

'Okay?' Any other time she would have felt embarrassed at the hysterical note she could hear in her voice, but now wasn't any other time. Ever since she had read the devastating news of Aggie's death, all she'd wanted to do was curl up in a ball in the safety of the cabin and cry out her grief. In private. Finding someone else here, claiming to be the new damn owner, was definitely not okay.

She glanced around the room, her eyes pin-pointing the jarring notes of change. The cabin was built on simple lines: to the right spread the living area, a book-lined space with tall windows flanking the riverstone fireplace. Usually those windows looked out at the valleys and mountains of the ranges – dizzying greens and sky blues in summer, rocky crags and white snow in winter. Not now. The dark had pressed in, nightfall hastened by a rapidly building weather front.

The man moved further in to the cabin, and she shrank back instinctively. The gun might have been put back in its holster, but its memory was still spread all over her mind's eye.

He sighed, and raised his hands in the air in a gesture she assumed was meant to forestall her alarm. 'I'm not going to attack you. I'm a cop. Ryan Mulligan, Detective with Sacramento PD. On holiday in my new cabin. I'm just going to light the fire before we freeze to death.'

'A cop?' So not an outlaw, or a movie star, or an ice hockey pro then. That explained the gun, if nothing else.

A dull whistle sounded from deep within the wide stack of the chimney – the wind was rising, and stray fingers of it were working their way down the flue, chilling the room. Aggie would never have let the fire go out at this time of year. And where were the quilts that should be stacked on the sofas? The lamplight spilling golden pools onto half-read paperbacks? The steam from a fresh-brewed mug of tea?

A thought struck her. 'Where's Mister Darcy?'

'Do me a favor, will you?' said the man. 'If you really knew the last owner of this place – can you turn the thermostat up? I've looked high and low and can't find the damn switch. Then you can tell me about you and this guy Darcy and we can work out whatever the hell is going on.'

The information was coming too thick and fast for her jet-lagged brain to keep up. *If* she knew the previous owner? What the hell did he mean by that?

The cop – Ryan – picked up his basket of kindling and moved over to the hearth, where he started feeding slabs of timber onto the cold ashes. She peeled her back off the front door and took a step into the room. To her left, a timber staircase spiralled up out of sight to the two bedrooms which filled the pointed attic, and beyond the stairs, flanking the back door, was the kitchen. No soup bubbled fragrantly on the cooker. No wildflowers bobbed their heavy heads from a scrubbed jam jar.

'Lady. You know where the thermostat is, or don't you?'

His voice interrupted her inspection of Aggie's kitchen. She looked across the room to where he stood before the fire, its fresh flames a silhouette of gold behind him like an aura in an early Christian painting. There was nothing angelic about the set of his face, however. He was eyeing her with about as much welcome as a winter virus.

She pursed her lips, sniffed, and marched to the low bench seat in the nook under the stairs. She wrestled with the upholstered cushion and the plywood sheet below until she'd exposed the cavity. Switches, gas knobs and utility meters clustered there, including the thermostat. She cranked its old-fashioned dial around to its usual winter setting, and heard the distant hum of the boiler in the cellar kick in.

If she knew the owner, indeed. She threw the cop a glance over her shoulder, raised her eyebrow in challenge.

Somebody needed to be giving her some answers, real soon.

***

The fire sent heat rushing through his extremities – he hadn't realized how cold he'd grown. Logs burst into orange and black spears of light, and he let the warmth play on his face for a second, before rising, and turning to face the problem he really didn't need who was standing in the middle of his new holiday cabin (which he'd damned well paid for) looking at him like he was a criminal.

Bloody hell. What next? Where did he have to hide to be

granted three damn seconds of alone time?

He rubbed his hand over the stubble he hadn't bothered shaving off. She was a looker though, this mystery girl with the tawny hair and the well-worn boots. May as well get it over with – whatever had to be done and said to send her on her way.

'Lisa, is it? You want a drink or something?'

She stayed planted in the middle of the room. 'I want to talk.'

'Yeah, okay. But I've just about frozen my ba— umm, my behind off chopping wood, so I'm having a coffee. It's no trouble to make two.'

She sighed. 'Sure. Just black, no sugar. Thank you.'

He filled the kettle under the tap and set it on the old-fashioned hob to come to the boil. Next trip up, he was bringing a normal kettle, one that plugged into a power socket. And a microwave. And thicker damn socks.

He kept an eye on his guest as he grabbed mugs from the drying rack. She'd pulled off her beanie and gloves, stuffing them into the pockets of her coat before that, too, came off. He watched, bemused, as she opened a paneled door under the stairs and hung her jacket in there on a hook. His hook. Where he'd have hung his own damn jacket if he'd known there was a hook there. The whistle of the kettle coming to the boil claimed his attention, and he filled two mugs then turned to face his guest.

Oh boy. Even his jaded cop eyes could appreciate the vision that stood before him. Unswaddled from her battered anorak, Lisa Wu was something else. Waves of hair the color of a mountain lion tumbled across her shoulders, down across her breast, falling to some low, low point behind her back that was making his imagination jump in ecstatic leaps.

A sprinkle of sand-colored freckles frisked across the pale skin of her cheeks. She was gorgeous. Her eyes were green, cat green, and her mouth ... he brought his inventory of her appearance to a ruthless halt. He hadn't escaped to the mountains to ogle women with beautiful eyes and tear-drenched lashes. He was here to be alone. Which he wasn't. A situation which needed to be remedied, fast.

'Kitchen table or fire?' he said, gesturing to the mugs in his hands.

In answer, Lisa pulled out a chair from the wooden table, pushing a bundle of newspapers to the side. His eye fell on the article she'd unwittingly shuffled to the top of the pile. *Sacramento's Hero: Detective Saves Strangler's Sixth Victim in Christmas Miracle.*

Hell's bells. He plonked a tin tub of chocolate-chip cookies down over the newsprint. He'd look forward to burning that article, along with any other he came across that featured him, later. Christmas miracle? Months of leg work, more like, following half-assed leads and one lucky break. He'd had about as much as he could take of the sensationalist headlines the *Sacramento Herald* persisted in printing.

'Cookie?'

She tipped the box in her direction and inspected the contents. 'These look – good.'

'Why the surprise?'

She shrugged, and picked out the biggest one in the tin. 'You don't look like much of a cookie baker.'

'Do I look like the spoiled and only son of a doting mother who does bake cookies?'

She looked up at him, the cookie half-bitten between her lips, and gave his face a once-over with those green-gold eyes, and he felt a burn start somewhere in his throat that spread over his skin like a rash. She finished her mouthful of cookie, and the longer he watched her eat it, the closer he came to forgetting what question he'd asked. He took a mental swipe at himself. Three days off the job and he'd forgotten how to interrogate someone? Get it together, Mulligan.

She didn't answer him, anyway. Instead, she placed on the table a bundle of letters. 'This feels so crazy, having to justify who I am, here, in Aggie's kitchen.'

Yeah. He could see that. She really had known where the thermostat was. The coat hook. She was genuinely upset to find him here, not angry, not thwarted in any way like an intruder would be. He reached a long arm behind him to the drawer below the breadbin and pulled out the folder he'd been given at the lawyer's office. He shook his head. 'I don't even know who Aggie is. Why don't you start, tell me your story, and I'll tell you mine.'

She nodded. 'Yes. Okay. Right. Aggie is Agatha Wendall, my grandmother. Her daughter Shona Wendall married Stanley Wu. They died in a car crash, oh, years ago now, but before they died, they adopted me. Aggie raised me after their death.'

'You want to tell me what's in that bundle?'

She placed a hand over the pile of letters protectively, as though she'd snatch them back if he were to make a move to grab them. The distrust pissed him off, and he wasn't sure why. But fine, he'd go first.

He pulled his contract out of its yellow legal envelope. The words *Jarrod Withers & Son, Attorneys At Law & Estate Planning*, shouted out in glossy print from the top of the page. His eyes flicked down to the salient part. *Seller: the estate of Agatha Wendall. Buyer: Ryan Mulligan.* He'd signed it – his black scrawl was its usual illegible mess on the dotted line. He read the seller's signature out loud: 'Jarrod Withers, Jr., Executor of the

Estate of Agatha Wendall.'

The lawyer's secretary had witnessed their signatures: a freckled youth who'd looked like he lived on a diet of soda and pastry, wearing a three-piece suit which hadn't seen a drycleaner in a tad too long. The contract looked legal to him. He swiveled it round so she could see for herself.

Her shoulders slumped as she read it, and he realized, belatedly, how tired she looked. Not that it was his problem. He was taking a break from problems. He'd earned it. He slugged down the rest of his cooling coffee. 'Maybe you'd better talk to the lawyer about your grandmother's estate. This Jarrod Junior must have the will, maybe you need to read it.'

She had her hands pressed to her face. He barely heard her when she spoke. 'I just can't believe it. Sold.'

Ryan looked at his watch. Spending his evening consoling a weeping stranger, even a beautiful one, was not high on his list. 'Yeah. Maybe he's working back late, you can catch him in his office when you get back to town.'

She dropped her hands to the table. 'Go?' she said, as though the word confused her.

He frowned. 'Yes. Go. As in pick up your bag, go outside, get in your car and go.'

She shook her head. 'I caught a cab up here. I don't own a car. I wasn't expecting to find some stranger had taken up residence in my home.'

Ryan didn't need complications. He needed alone time. 'No car. How were you expecting to leave again? Buy food? There's no shops in walking distance.'

She frowned. 'We're in the mountains, not the moon. I'd call the cab company to come get me.'

'No mobile phone reception. I've checked.'

'Mobiles don't work, sure, but the landline does …

unless—'

'That's right, lady. Disconnected. Seems like our lawyer friend Mr Withers has been very diligent tidying up loose ends like utilities.'

'Oh god.' The words sighed out of her on a little shudder.

Nope, his evening was definitely not working out as planned. Strapping chains onto his tires in the freezing cold versus chugging down beer in front of the fire? Resigned, he made the offer. 'Come on, I'll give you a lift. My car's parked out back.'

A pellet spray of ice and sleet chose that moment to rat-a-tat-tat across the windows of the cabin, and beneath the noise, building in a rumble that seemed to echo through the crags and peaks of the mountainside, rolled a long and ominous sound of thunder.

'That doesn't sound good.'

'Yeah.' He stood up and moved to the back door, opening it so he could see the sky. He was startled to see how much snow had fallen since he'd been inside having an ownership contest with his uninvited guest. High winds were whipping mini tornadoes in the clearing behind the house, and his car was axle deep in snow.

He'd not be driving anywhere tonight – not on strange roads through a full-blown mountain storm.

Lisa's voice sounded behind him. 'I think we're snowed in.'

A deep crack sounded in the distance, and he jumped, his hand rocketing to the gun holstered to his chest. What the hell?

The noise sounded again, but duller this time, and he narrowed his gaze on the door of the woodshed, which was being pushed outward against the snow piled up on it from outside, as though someone inside was battering at it to get out.

The door thumped a third and final time, and a black shape shifted against the snow, then barreled towards him in the open doorway. Behind him, he heard Lisa cry out. His gun was halfway out of his holster and he was flexing his thigh muscles, poised to act, in the instant before his brain registered the truth.

'Mister Darcy!' he heard Lisa exclaim, in the same moment he thought *the stray.*

A black Labrador the size of a school bus lumbered past his legs, through the open doorway, and launched itself at Lisa who was on her knees on the kitchen floor, crying and laughing and looking as though she'd just discovered the meaning of Christmas.

He felt his heart spin a mini-tornado of its own in his chest.

***

Lisa buried her face in the ruff of the dog's neck. His fur was cold but in deep, where fur ended and a writhing, wagging, happy dog body commenced, he was warm. She let his ruff soak up some of the emotion that had been threatening to overwhelm her all day, then gathered his big boofhead in her hands.

'Mister Darcy. Where have you been?'

The kitchen door closed with a thunk, locking out the bitter wind, and she looked up at Ryan as he shoved home the bolt then turned to regard her with a bemused look in his eye.

She raised an eyebrow. 'What is it?'

He let out a laugh, and the change it wrought over his face pulled her out of her fog of tiredness. She forgot where she was and spoke without thinking. 'You should smile more often.'

He acknowledged the comment with a nod of his head. 'You're probably right. You want to tell me who the hell this great black lump is?'

She rose to her feet, giving Mister Darcy a last stroke between the ears as she did so. The dog then tottered over to the fire, collapsing in a heap on the rug with a groan of contentment. Clearly, the dog wasn't bothered at all by Ryan's presence in Aggie's cabin ... maybe she could learn from that. She risked a smile at her unwilling host.

'Mister Darcy is Aggie's dog. She usually leaves him with the vet when she's away. Toby. Have you met him yet? He owns a ranch further down the mountain, maybe twenty minutes' walk if you take the hiking track out back.'

Ryan shook his head. 'Nope. But I've seen the dog. He's turned up a time or two. Nosed around, accepted a corned beef sandwich and disappeared again. I thought he was a stray.'

'He must be living at Toby's place, wondering when Aggie will be by to collect him.'

'Mmm.'

'So, I guess you've got two guests for the night,' she said. And she'd be taking Mister Darcy up to her bedroom with her when she went upstairs. As fierce guard dogs went, he was about as useful as a hockey sock, but he was one big guy. If he slept against her door, it would take more than one tough-jawed, sexy-eyed cop to push it open.

Sexy-eyed? Where had that daft thought come from? Lisa shook her head. She needed to get her emotions back under control. She was in no state to be having wild thoughts about handsome strangers.

Ryan seemed to have resigned himself to having had his quiet evening turned upside down. 'Yeah. The storm's too bad to risk the road. And who am I to deny a dog a warm spot in front of a fire? It is Christmas eve, after all. Not the night to be turning strangers from the stable, to borrow a phrase.'

Christmas eve! In all the drama of the day she'd lost track.

***

'So.' Lisa cleared her throat. The chill in the room had evaporated as the fire took hold, and its crackle and flickering light filled the room. Outside, the storm had picked up a notch, the wind outside making a high-pitched roar.

Snow was piling up on the wide windowsills, building a barrier between her and the world outside – between her and her job, Aggie's grave that she hadn't yet visited, her past, her future.

Here, in the cabin, she was cocooned with warmth. The sounds reminded her of her childhood: snow buffeting the window panes, logs crackling, even the deep rumble of Mister Darcy's snore.

But there was change, too – the six foot, living breathing evidence of which was currently lounging across the other sofa, filling way more space than Aggie ever had. She settled deeper into the down cushions, reflecting on how she felt to be sharing her cocoon with a guy. A handsome one, whose face could turn from tough to warm in an instant.

It was almost – she felt color flood her cheeks, but finished the thought anyway – romantic.

'This is a bit awkward,' she said, to stop herself dwelling on inappropriate ideas of romance. 'Having to stay here, I mean. With you.'

'Don't sweat it. There's a spare room, I've got food. We can drive into town in the morning and go tackle Jarrod Withers Junior in his office together.'

'You're forgetting something. Tomorrow is Christmas Day. His office will be shut.'

'Crap. I was forgetting that.' Ryan sighed. 'Look, I've had a hell of a few weeks – why don't we just worry about tomorrow, tomorrow. I'm about ready for a beer and a steak.'

A woof sounded from the rug before the fireplace. Lisa smiled. 'It's a good plan. Mister Darcy is very fond of steak. Why don't I cook, since you bought the food?'

Ryan grinned, a long slow grin that had her understanding why his mum continued to bake chocolate chip cookies for him. 'That's the best thing I've heard all day,' he said. 'You want a beer?'

She wrinkled her nose. 'No. There might be some wine in the cellar. Have you been down there yet?'

Ryan walked to the fridge and pulled out a brown bottle. He cracked its top and took a swig. 'Honey, I didn't even know there *was* a cellar.'

'Trap door under the stairs. There's an outside entry too, but it'll be frozen over at this time of year. I'll get the dinner on then go investigate.'

'Sounds like a plan. You want a hand? I could, maybe, chop something?'

She smiled at his offer. About an hour ago, she'd been horrified to find some big stranger cluttering up her alone time in Aggie's cabin. But now? With the warm fire, the snoring dog, the promise of a home cooked meal and a little company that was easy on the eye? Her breath hitched a little as she realized what this felt like. It felt a little like not being lonely.

'You relax,' she said. 'I could do with a bit of time pottering in the kitchen. If you don't mind.'

He nodded. 'Take your time. I'll go have a shower then share the fire with that great smelly lump you call a dog.'

***

The temperature in the van was bitter as fuck, but instead of cooling Elliott Fox down, it just added fuel to his fire of rage. Four goddamn hours it had taken him, driving here from Sacramento. And days before that trying to work out where the fuck that cop Mulligan had gotten to.

Run like a girl, that's what he'd done. And his bimbo mother so stupid she'd stuck his hidey-hole address up on her fridge. Shame she'd been out when he went calling. He'd have hung around to squeeze her neck if he hadn't been in a hurry.

Elliott giggled, and a spray of saliva arced from his mouth and landed on the stained corduroy of his pants. Dumb cop couldn't take the fame, so he'd scarpered. Fame was for the brave, thought Elliot. For people like him, who saw what they wanted, and took it, and enjoyed the wave of notoriety and fear that followed.

He tapped another Adderall from the glass bottle into his palm and washed it down with whiskey. He'd had four since the cloud came down and covered the sun, and he was feeling juiced on the buzz. First time he'd felt this good since Mulligan took down Tate.

No. Couldn't think of that. Tonight he had work to do. If he started getting his tits in a tangle about Tate, he'd lose focus. Tonight was about making the cop pay.

He opened the sliding door wide enough to prop himself in the doorway and piss. A yellow stream pulsed out into the snow, and an icy wind snuck in past him, through him, ruffling the papers and cable ties and tools he had readied. He cast a wary eye out over the thrashing trees and wild sleet. He'd be needing the storm to die down a mite for him to get his game on later tonight.

But he had a good feeling. The buzz in his brain was telling him not to worry. Everything was going to go his way tonight, the way it always did.

Finished, he zipped himself back into his pants and slid the van door shut as quietly as he could. He doubted anyone was in hearing distance especially with the wind out there screaming like a cut whore – but he didn't take chances. Which was why he was out here, free as a birdy, while Tate was holed up in some federal high security prison getting shivs jammed up his ass by his cellmates.

No. Couldn't think of that. Focus, focus, *focus*.

He pulled the three-day-old paper out from under his gun and read the headline again. *Sacramento's Hero: Detective Saves Strangler's Sixth Victim in Christmas Miracle*. He giggled, enjoying the joke. The cop had been wrong. The newspaper had been wrong. Everyone had got it so fucking wrong. Because there wasn't just one strangler, was there?

There'd been two. Him and Tate. Because where was the fun in stalking your victim, waiting until you could smell their fear, wrapping your cool gloved fingers around their jerking, shuddering necks, if you didn't have someone to share the game with?

He clapped his hands. Tate had screwed up, big time, getting himself caught, but Elliott had a plan. He was going to bring about a Christmas fucking miracle of his own. Let the *Sacramento Herald* write about that!

He sang a little under his breath, because, really, this was his best game ever. He was going to take a sixth victim for real this time – and when the stupid journalists realized that the sixth victim was the very cop who'd been prancing around like a city hero saying no-one would ever get strangled again – well, that would show them all.

He rattled the bottle of pills, wondering if he could risk another. Better not. He could celebrate later, when Mulligan's neck was a lifeless sausage between his hands. When Tate had been found not guilty, because hey, whaddayouknow, he was locked up when the hero cop got whacked.

Elliott looked at his watch. Nine o'clock. He'd wait a few hours yet. Give the weather time to die down, and his prey to get sleepy. He stroked a hand over the tools he'd need for later: gun, backpack, cable ties, head torch, balaclava, hunting jacket. Then he settled down to wait.

He started to hum a snatch of song and giggled as he sang the words. *'Tis the season to be jolly, fa la la la la, la la la la* ...

***

Lisa leaned against the high back of the old church pew that served as seating on one side of the kitchen table. She felt ... relaxed. And despite the sadness that lingered, the simple task of preparing a meal, scrubbing spuds in Aggie's sink, remembering the trick to lighting the old stove – these homely acts had been cathartic.

And the solid presence of Ryan wolfing down his steak and baked potatoes and greens had been heartwarming too. Especially since he'd left his gun upstairs after his shower. Sitting opposite her, his eyes crinkling with amusement, his dark hair damp and spiking every which way, he looked less like a cop and more like a ... well, man.

She'd had company on the giant clam project on Aitutaki. In the shared accommodation there'd always been chatting, work discussions, the twang of an acoustic guitar being plucked by the off-duty cook. But as team leader, she'd felt a responsibility to maintain a demarcation between her and the other researchers.

She'd joined in the fun when time permitted, taken the student volunteers on snorkeling trips through the lagoon, fired the moron who thought harassing the junior aquaculturist was his god given right ...

But she'd not made a close friend during her time in the Cook Islands. Certainly not one who made her heart pound in the thrilling way it was pounding now.

The reason for her pounding heart was currently sliding a look sideways at Mister Darcy, who had spent dinnertime staring at them both mournfully, projecting an air of imminent death from starvation. 'What an actor,' said Ryan. 'He's got enough fat on him to hibernate in a cave for six months.'

She grinned. 'He certainly had Aggie under his thumb. Well, paw.'

'Mm. Speaking of Aggie ...' Ryan rested his hand briefly on top of hers where it lay beside the plate, and squeezed gently. She felt her beat of attraction slide up an octave. 'How are you feeling?'

She'd read him the letters over dinner. Explained how devastated she had been to have been on the other side of the world when Aggie died. She'd cried again – she was really going to have to work on that. And he'd not baulked even when she read the part about the new will. Instead, he'd offered to help her ransack the hundreds of books lining the cabin's floor to ceiling shelves. They'd made a start on the books by the fire, and found shopping lists and pressed flowers and embroidered bookmarks that looked like they came from the nineteenth century. But they had not found the will, not yet.

She cleared her throat and felt a rush of heat sliding up her cheeks. She wasn't sure if she was sad or relieved when he took his hand away. 'I feel tired. Emotional. Jetlagged.' She managed a smile. 'But, actually, talking it all through has kind of helped. Thank you.'

He nodded, and pulled her plate over to his side of the table. 'You cooked. I'll wash up. You never did have that glass of wine you wanted. Why don't you go relax while I sort out the kitchen?'

What a marvelous idea. A glass of wine, then she'd rug up and take the dog out to do his business, before heading upstairs to the attic room that had been hers since she was a child. She felt like she could sleep for a month.

The trapdoor behind the stairwell was stiff, and it took her a few tugs of the handle to lift the heavy door. She dropped to her knees and felt around through the dark hole until she felt the thin cord of the pull switch. A dull yellow light clicked on, filling the dusty space below her, lighting up the steep ladder that led downwards. She swiveled around, and cautiously descended into the gloom. She'd forgotten how cold it was in the cellar – how much it felt like descending into a tomb. She shivered at the nonsensical thought.

She hadn't been in the cellar in ages ... two years? Three? Her eyes took a while to reacquaint themselves with the layout. A stack of tea crates filled with books lined the southern wall, beside them a narrow ramp which led up to the cellar's main entry point, outside in the garden.

Shelves filled the opposite wall, jumbled with spanners and old shower curtain hooks, and something that looked suspiciously like an old bakelite rotary dial telephone. She huffed. The phone was an antique, probably from the bookstore Aggie had run before she retired, and deemed worthless along with everything else in the cabin by Jarrod

Withers Junior. She pressed her fingers into the smooth circles above each digit, imagined Aggie's fingers resting there while she called her mum, her customers, maybe even a much-spoiled adopted grandchild.

She blew a cloud of dust off a pile of books jumbled into the nearest crate. She'd forgotten how many there were. Her thoughts traveled to the line she'd read out to Ryan from Aggie's letter: *it's in a book, pressed between two of my favorite pages. Now if only I could remember which book.* She'd finish checking the ones upstairs first. It was too cold now, in the dead of night, to stand among these crates and the memories of Aggie that lingered with them.

A cluster of dusty bottles caught her eye. Aha! She knew she'd seen wine down here. She held a few labels up to the light, but time and damp had eroded the descriptions. Oh well. She didn't mind surprises, so long as they were good ones. She'd just have to open one and hope for the best.

She turned back to the ladder and spied an old polystyrene fruit carton tucked to the side, red and gilt baubles glistening in the light from the naked bulb. Christmas decorations! Should she take some upstairs? She had begun the day feeling like she never wanted to hear the word Christmas again ... but would it hurt to bring a little festivity into her life? Aggie wouldn't have thought so, she was all for seizing the moment.

She dropped to her knees and started rootling through the carton. Tinsel rolls spilled out, along with spiky bundles of fairy lights, and deep within she found a wreath of dried mistletoe hung with white glass berries. 'Oh,' she breathed. She and Aggie had made this wreath, years before, for her first Christmas after her new parents had died. She'd been seven? Eight?

She'd only been adopted by the Wu family a few months

before the car crash that claimed their lives. Before that, she'd been in foster care. She'd barely known her new mum and dad, let alone this eccentric lady who she'd now come to live with, who baked and recited poetry and knit exotic tea cozies.

But they'd collected the thin branches together, out there on the slopes of the mountain, wound them into the wreath, and hung it on the front door. *Now everyone who comes to visit will know a family lives here*, Aggie had said. *Do you mean us*, she could remember her child self asking. Worrying. Aggie had hugged her so hard she squealed. *Yes, us. You and me. We're a family now.*

She carefully eased the wreath from the box. It was practically an antique too. She was just turning to find the bottle of wine she'd put down on the floor, when the light from the bulb above her snapped out.

The dark was absolute. She strained to hear the boiler humming away but it, too, was silent. A deep voice sounded above her.

'Lisa? I think the power's gone out.'

Crap. She gripped the wreath in one hand and the bottle of wine in the other. 'Can you remember seeing a torch anywhere?'

'Yeah. There's one in my car. There's another one under the sink in my apartment in Sacramento. Neither of them easy to reach right now.'

What a smartass. She edged in the direction where she thought the ladder was, and winced as her shin collected the corner of a tea chest. 'Umm, Ryan?'

His voice was closer. 'Yep?'

'I can't find the ladder.'

There was a laugh in his voice as he responded. 'Hang on. There's a box of matches near the fire. If I can make my way there without tripping over Mister Darcy.'

'Be careful,' she called up. 'You can't see him in the dark, he's too black.'

'Yeah, but I can hear him. He's snoring like a lawnmower. And I think he's moved onto the couch.'

She laughed. 'He's not allowed on the couch.'

Ryan's voice was closer again, and a wavering light appeared overhead. 'I don't think he agreed to that rule. Hang on, I'm coming down.'

The match flickered out, and she heard creaking as Ryan's feet planted themselves on the timber slatted ladder. Resting the bottle in the crate she'd walked into, she reached out in the dark to find the wall of the cellar, and found her hand resting on a warm, firm, wool-covered male chest.

'I guess I found you.' Ryan's voice had dropped to a breath above a whisper.

Take your hand off him, she urged herself. But her hand seemed to have developed a will of its own. It slid, gently, down an inch, two, feeling the curve and furrow of muscle and rib.

The scratch of a match against the sandpaper of its box was the only sound in the cellar, and a yellow flame suddenly lit the air between them. Ryan's face was close, his shadowed jaw an inch or two above hers, his dark eyes resting on her face. She took in a shuddering breath. *You are crazy*, her rational brain was saying. *Crazy, crazy, crazy.*

She didn't care. Was it the jetlag? The emotional rollercoaster of her day? The unrecognized heat that had started to burn for this brooding-eyed man from the second she'd laid eyes on him, standing there in Aggie's kitchen with a gun in his hand and a don't-mess-with-me-I'm-at-the-end-of-my-tether look on his face? None of that mattered. She just knew she was going to kiss him, here, in the dusty cellar, with a mistletoe wreath she'd made as a child clutched in her hand.

She kept her eyes on his. 'I'm just going to do one thing.' Then she leaned up and pressed her mouth to his.

***

Holy smokes, she was going to kiss hi—

That was his last rational thought before instinct took over. Her mouth landed on his, but if she was giving he was taking. He shook the flame out before the match burned down to his fingers, but he doubted he would have felt it. The rest of him had lit up like a bonfire when those green eyes of hers had locked on his, drenched with need and lust and wonder.

He was feeling a bunch of that need and lust and wonder himself. He wrapped an arm around her to bring her closer, so he could feel the length of her from tip to toe. He dropped the box of matches, not caring that without them they were blind down here in the dark, and wrapped his free hand in among the long swathes of her hair so he could fuse himself to her.

She moaned, or was it him? Her lips were moving under his, and her hand was running up his side, skimming under his sweater, and holy Christ her nails were blazing a trail like burning liquor up his torso because he couldn't remember how to breathe.

When had he last been kissed like this? When had he last felt this kick of urgent, searing need? When had he last been anything more than a cop drowning in the demands of his job?

He wanted more. He wanted to see, feel, taste. He wanted the heat, but he wanted comfort with it. Sex *and* solace. He broke away from her mouth, needing to explore, and ran his lips down the side of her neck, across her collarbone. She was wearing some fussy sort of jumper, with too much fabric, way too much fabric, covering way too much of her. If he could just reach under and—

A deep insistent woof from over his head snapped him out of the spell she'd wrapped him in, and he placed an urgent finger over her mouth. Not even a kiss that blistered like that one had could dull his cop instincts. That hadn't sounded like a happy bark.

She murmured against his fingers. 'It's nothing. Maybe more thunder coming. Mister Darcy is scared of storms.'

Something foul was stirring in his gut, and he'd been a cop too long to ignore it. Playtime was over. Reluctantly, he slid his hands from Lisa's warm body. 'I don't like it. Let's get upstairs. I dropped the matches.'

He knelt down, and Lisa knelt with him, their elbows and knees bumping as they scrambled in the dark for the box. His fingers rasped over the rough surface, and he lit a match, just as the dog above them rumbled out a low, menacing growl.

'That's not like him,' Lisa said. 'I've never heard him growl.'

Where was his fucking gun? Upstairs under his pillow, like a damn nightgown. He lifted the match high before it burned out, getting the steps to the ladder measured out in his head. His eyes caught on an old jam jar wedged in the corner of the bottom step – a jam jar with a stub of candle in it. He lit a new match, and held it to the wick. 'Any more of these lying around?'

'I'll find them. Leave the matches with me and I'll bring some up. You check on the dog.'

He didn't need to be told twice. The churn in his gut was spiking his adrenalin, and being blind in a cellar was almost as frustrating as being without his holster and weapon. He ran up the ladder, then turned to see the dog standing on the window seat, bathed in firelight, his nose pressed to the glass and his hackles erect. He breathed a small sigh. At least whatever the problem was, it was outside. First job was getting some lights on in this place. He threw a couple more logs on the fire, then went to the trapdoor, where he could see Lisa had found a bunch of candle stubs in jars and was passing them up one by one.

She climbed out of the hole, and he gave her a hand easing the trapdoor shut again. 'Whatever's spooked him is outside. Can you keep watch for a second? I'm going upstairs to get my gun.'

'Your gun? Ryan.' She was smiling at him like he was a toddler who'd just suggested he'd like fairy floss for dinner. 'It's probably a squirrel. Or a tree's come down in the wind.'

'The storm's quietening down. I don't think it was a tree, Lisa.' He went up the stairs. She could talk about squirrels and trees all she liked, she wasn't a cop. She didn't know what went on in the dark places of the world. He'd be getting his gun and checking things out and if he was overreacting, that was fine. They could laugh about it in the morning.

Lisa had a pot on the stove when he came downstairs, and the rich aroma of warm wine and oranges and spices filled the air. 'Gas stovetop,' she said, correctly reading the look of enquiry on his face.

'So power outages are common then,' he said, relieved to hear it was unlikely someone was outside messing with the power supply. He kept one eye on the dog, who'd given up his post at the window and now lay across the kitchen floor, like a rug, only way, way fatter.

'I figured I'd make some mulled wine.'

She seemed a little shy, and turned back to the stove. No wonder. If the dog hadn't interrupted them, heaven only knows where that hot-handed tryst in the cellar would have ended up. He tamped down the thought. 'I'm going to get my torch from the car, have a look around.'

She shot him a look over her shoulder. 'Are you really worried about something? Ryan, there's no need. Aggie's never had any trouble up here, and she was here thirty years.'

'No harm in making sure.' He looked at Mister Darcy. 'I'll take the old boy out with me. He can pee on my car tires and keep me company.'

She let out a snort of laughter. 'He'd like that.'

Ryan shrugged his way into his jacket and pulled on the grey beanie and gloves he'd brought downstairs with him. 'Lock the door after me. Don't let anyone in but me.'

She looked bemused, but she did as he asked. The last he saw of her was her green cat eyes watching him through the glass pane of the back door, her hair shimmering in the candlelight.

***

Lisa turned the gas off under the pan. She found an old aluminum lid in the cupboard under the sink, so plonked it on top to keep the mulled wine warm. Maybe they could sit by the fire and have a nightcap when Ryan came back inside.

She felt a blush running up under her skin. Ryan. The rollercoaster of her day just kept throwing in more loops. She ran a wet cloth over the scrubbed timber of the table, gathering up the orange pips and cinnamon grinds she'd spilled there. Aggie's recipe. Aggie's kitchen. She smiled, wondered if Aggie was up in heaven somewhere, looking down, smiling at the wild day her granddaughter had ended up having.

An orange pip had rolled in under the cluster of newspapers Ryan had bundled at the far end of the table, and she flicked the pages to the side to pinch the errant pip up between her fingertips. A black and white picture splashed over the folded page of newsprint caught her eye. Was that *Ryan?*

She unfolded the paper and sat down on the pew, her eyes growing wider as she read.

Ryan Mulligan, an experienced detective with the Sacramento Police Department, has apprehended the serial killer known as the Strangler, after a six-month investigation and five confirmed fatalities. The sixth victim, an international student just nineteen years of age, was rescued from the Strangler's clutches before her life, too, could be taken. The arrest of 46-year-old Tate Collingwood followed ...

Lisa's eyes galloped down the page as she read the finer details, including reports of the personal toll the ferocity of the crime scenes had taken on the police officers on the investigative team. That poor man! No wonder he couldn't relax. Here she was, plotting red wine and canoodling on a rug in front of a fire, and Ryan was out there in the freezing cold because he was so wired up. She'd been so caught up in her feelings, she'd not taken a moment to wonder about his.

He'd been so good about her turning up out of the blue and announcing there was a will that would muddy the ownership waters of the cabin he'd just bought, and now he was freezing his fine-looking face off because he was worried about noises in the woods. She should go out there and help him do his perimeter check or whatever it was he thought he needed to do, not be sitting in here. She was no useless missy; she'd grown up in this wilderness.

She stood up and peered through the glass, but it was pitch black. No starlight split the view into snow and trees. No moonlight glimmered on the mountain peaks. She could see nothing.

She rested her fingers on the lock, but her promise to Ryan rang in her mind. Lock the door. Don't let anyone in but him. She rested her head against the glass. Where was he? Surely he'd have circled the house by now? She rushed over to the tall windows either side of the fireplace. He'd been going to collect his torch, so why couldn't she see its cone of light flickering through the trees?

She rubbed her hands up her arms. She was freaking out now – and she'd never been freaked out up here. This was her safe place, damn it. Just as she was berating herself for being such a scaredy cat, an urgent wave of ferocious barking tore through the night.

Mister Darcy! His deep voice boomed, then cut off with a shrill yelp and then—nothing.

She froze. Waited one second, two. 'Oh god, oh god, oh god,' she breathed. If she was scared before, she was terrified now. Where were they? What had happened to the dog?

She heard a thump at the back door and jumped. Thank god. He was back. She raced over, thinking ahead to admitting how foolish she'd been being worried, but here they both were, the wine still warm ...

But then a black gloved fist punched through the glass pane in the back door and a hand reached down, slid the lock, and the door opened.

She stood, the back of her legs pressed to the sofa, her limbs frozen with fear. A man stood in the doorway, dressed completely in black, his face hidden behind a balaclava.

He had a gun in one hand, and in the other – oh no, surely it wasn't? He dropped the blue leather strap to the floor, where its buckle and name tag glittered in the flickering light. Mister

Darcy's collar.

Bile rushed up through her gut. 'Who are you?' she whispered. Did he know about Ryan, out there circling the house? Was Ryan safe? Or had this man got to him the way he'd got to Mister Darcy?

He giggled – a girlish sound that sent a chill through her veins. And then he slammed the door shut behind him and rammed the bolt home. He took off his balaclava, and she was faced with a pink-cheeked man who would have looked like a middle-aged cherub, but for the glitter of madness in his eyes, and the string of wetness which hung, trembling, from his lip.

'Who am I?' He seemed delighted to be asked. He waved his gun at her indicating she move towards him. She shook her head. She'd rather be shot than go any closer to the madman at the door.

'Now now, my pet, don't be shy. There's no point waiting all the way over there. Detective Mulligan won't be coming in to rescue you any time.' The man laughed, gleefully. 'He's a little tied up.'

He knew Ryan's name? This was no chance encounter then. Her eyes flew to the newspaper she had been reading, which still lay across the kitchen table. The man's gaze followed hers, and when his eyes fell on the half page photograph of Ryan, he bared his teeth in a feral grin that showed no amusement.

'So full of himself,' he said in his sing-song voice. 'So sure he'd nabbed me.'

Nabbed me? The man wasn't making any sense.

'But he didn't know everything, did he? Oh yes, he got Tate. And it was a blow. I'd trained Tate up to be a most excellent assistant.'

Assistant? The terror overtaking Lisa clawed its way up her throat, and she struggled to breathe. The man Ryan had arrested in Sacramento, the serial killer, hadn't been working alone. The other Strangler was here, in her grandmother's cabin, waving a gun at her, and she had no way to run.

'Now. Enough playing around.' The man had stopped giggling. His words lashed out like a whip crack. 'To the table, or I shoot you in the knee.'

Lisa inched forward, on limbs stiff with fear and cold. The temperature in the cabin had plummeted with the broken glass knocked out of the window, and her roll neck sweater was no protection against the cold.

She needed a weapon. A tool. But the table was bare but for newspapers, and the sofa behind her was a pillow strewn place of comfort, not a workbench. The only weapon she had was herself. She had an education, she had skills. Now was the time she had to hope those skills paid off. She had to slow him down long enough for an opportunity to present itself. She was nobody's victim.

'So you have an opening for a new assistant?' she said, trying not to gag on the words. 'Perhaps I should share my resume with you. Did you know I'm a scientist?'

***

Ryan came to with the metal of blood in his mouth and fury burning through his veins. He'd been taken out with a wire strung between trees at knee height, and then clubbed in the head with something heavy. Might have been a gun butt, but his skull felt like he'd been clobbered by a giant swinging a forklift.

So much for man's best friend. There was no sign of Mister Darcy. He struggled to lift his hands from the weight of snow pinning him to the ground to check his gun, then realized he was tied up, his hands wrist to wrist, then a loop attaching him to his feet, tied ankle to ankle.

His brain refuted the facts. How could he be tied up in the exact manner the Strangler used to tie his victims before he killed them? He'd arrested the killer. That lowlife was behind bars of cold-forged steel a couple hundred miles away.

He didn't believe in coincidence. Someone had followed him up here into the mountains and taken him out. Taken his gun too, for fuck's sake. But why? If the person who'd knocked him out was, as unlikely as it could be, in cahoots with the Strangler, why not kill him? Why leave him tied up in the snow?

His heart missed a beat as he pictured Lisa, waiting for him in the cabin. With no phone. No internet. And no clue of the danger which might be coming her way. Maybe this intruder preferred a younger, better looking victim than a cop unconscious in the snow.

He didn't understand what was going on, not yet. A copycat killer? A prison breakout? His mind was buzzing with combinations and permutations. But he was going to find out. Light shone between tree trunks, so he couldn't be far from the cabin. If he could find the wood shed, he could find the axe he'd left sunk into the block. And with an axe, he'd be back in the race.

He swung awkwardly to his feet, hoping he wasn't too late. Moving was awkward through the snow. Thanking his lucky stars for the gym work he put in every week, he edged closer to the light. He was at the rear of the house, which was his first break – the chopping block was close.

Ignoring the pain from the tight wire binding his ankles, he kept up the shuffle through the snow drifts. Not much further. He skirted the dark side of his parked car, wishing like hell he had a rifle in there, a radio back to HQ, anything more useful than the detritus of empty coffee cups rolling round the footwell.

The shadow of the woodshed rose from the snow before him, and he turned his shoulder into it, brushing at the snowfall. He smiled, grimly, with no humor. Woodshed, chopping block, axe. Now he had a chance. He forced his bound hands against the honed steel of the blade buried amid the snow on the block and commenced sawing. 'Come on,' he whispered. 'Come *on*.'

Finally, the tension forcing his wrists into their unnatural position snapped. He was free. He ripped off his gloves so he could work on the knots keeping his feet hogtied, then hefted the axe from its block.

Hang on Lisa. I'm coming.

He crept to the back door, leaned up against it, risked a quick look through the broken pane of its glass. Lisa was alive. Tied to the chair at the end of the kitchen table, but upright, unharmed. Pale, but coping. He willed her to look his way, but her eyes were wide, staring into the hidden corner of the kitchen.

He held the axe, poised to smash it against the lock holding the back door shut, but then a man clad in black moved across the narrow space of the door's broken window. He had a gun in his hand, another, Ryan's own police issue colt, poking out of the pocket of his anorak. Shit. If he leapt in, there was no telling where that gun would be pointed.

He hesitated, working through his options, and his frantic thoughts were interrupted as the words of the man who had tied Lisa up in her grandmother's kitchen drifted through the window.

'Oh sure, your manfriend arrested Tate. But he was never

more than my tool. My acolyte. How foolish your detective was, to think he'd halted the Strangler. No-one can halt me. No-one can arrest me.'

A high giggle cleaved the frozen air, and Ryan's blood iced over. Visions of the crime scenes he'd processed played across his mind. Not one serial killer, but two! Working as a team. How could he have missed it?

He had to gain entry to the cabin and come up behind the madman. But how? The front door was deadlocked, he'd made sure of that earlier. Breaking a window would destroy his element of surprise. He had an axe, but an axe needed proximity. It was no use across a room against a hand gun.

A flicker of memory jolted him. What had Lisa said? *Trap door under the stairs. There's an outside entry too, but it'll be frozen over at this time of year.* He didn't care how frozen it was, he was getting the hell in. Bending low so his head remained out of sight, and placing his feet carefully to minimize the sound of his boots crunching through the snow, he headed round to the side of the house. The cellar doors must be somewhere.

Thank Christ he'd had those few moments in the cellar – the ones before Lisa wrapped herself around him and his brain stopped functioning. He had a clear picture of the ramp down there and it's gradient. Keeping a hand on the rough exterior of the cabin to guide him, he sprinted along its stone wall. He was in luck. A ragged hedge skirted the footings of the cabin, abruptly stopping for a five-foot-wide gap. *Gotcha.* Planting his legs, he swung the blunt end of the axe down through the snow and heard the dull thunk of wood shifting.

He'd found the cellar doors. Now he needed to clear them. Snow had been falling steadily for hours, and he had no idea how big an area he had to uncover, but he didn't stop to think, he just dropped to his knees and began sweeping large swathes of it away. Close in to the timber, ice had formed and he chiseled at it with the blade of the axe until it cracked.

His frozen fingers finally found what they were looking for: two huge iron rings shifted heavily as he worked at them, and he wedged his hands into them, stood so he could use his weight as leverage, and pulled for all his might.

The doors groaned in protest, but then opened. *Here goes.* He stepped forward into the gaping black hole.

If he thought it had been dark outside, he'd been kidding himself. Stepping into the cellar was like being buried alive. He threw aside the image. Lisa needed him, and she needed him now.

The deeper he traveled, the clearer the muffled voices above him began. A man's voice, going on and on – and then, yes, definitely a female response. She was still alive.

He spread his hands out, seeking for the ladder that would bring him to the trapdoor. If he were to fumble now, or crash into the crates of wine bottles stored down here, his element of surprise would be destroyed. And besides the axe, and determination, surprise was all he had.

His thoughts turned in a circle – from Lisa, her face in the candlelight, staring up at him in that breathless second before she'd kissed him – to the faces of the five victims he'd been too late to save in the Strangler's Sacramento killing spree.

He'd been so sure Tate Collingwood was the Strangler. His DNA was all over the victims. Their DNA was all over his station wagon. And he'd not had a whiff of suspicion that an accomplice was involved in any of the crimes; not a hair, not a phone record, not a thumb print.

Whoever the guy was holding Lisa upstairs, he was smart. Cunning.

At last, the tips of his outstretched fingers made contact

with the rough wood of the ladder, and he gripped it. Hefting the axe with his other hand, he began climbing. He had to face the monster who'd slipped through his investigation like a ghost through time. But more than that, he had to rescue Lisa, the woman who'd landed in his life due to a misunderstanding and thrown his well-ordered senses into heat-fueled chaos. He had to climb up and rescue his future.

***

Lisa knew the madman was going to choke her. Oh, he'd enjoyed his posturing, strutting about the kitchen telling her how clever he was, how devious, with his games and tools and prey.

But he wasn't interested in listening to her. When she flinched as he leaned forward over the table, his meaty hands splayed before her on the wood, she'd seen the excitement flicker in his eyes.

He wanted her to be afraid. That's what he enjoyed. He wasn't giving her time so she could reason with him and walk away. He was giving her time to grow from scared, to terrified, to paralyzed with fear.

And it was working. She felt utterly, utterly helpless. Her hands were tied behind her back. Her feet were wedged apart and cable-tied to the legs of the table. The man, who had introduced himself as Elliott Fox, had slipped his gun into a pocket of his hunting jacket, but not before he'd waved Ryan's gun before her eyes.

'You manfriend was my game tonight, but that was before I knew about you.'

He walked behind her and ran a finger over the side of her neck. She tried not to flinch – every time she did, his speech grew rushed and he appeared more excited.

'But there you were, cozying up indoors, and I had a lightbulb moment. You know what I'm saying?'

She tried to sound calm, like she was in a meeting discussing plankton levels and rising sea temperatures, rather than engaging in small talk with a serial killer. 'You had a bright idea.'

He clapped his hands. 'No-one plays the game as well as Elliott Fox. My idea wasn't bright, it was brilliant. Mulligan took Tate from me. And now I can take you from him.'

Her breath stuttered on these words. Did that mean Ryan wasn't dead? Just incapacitated out there in the snow? She shot a look out the windows, to the dark nothing outside. The temperature had to be below freezing. Was he unconscious? Bleeding? Restrained, like she was? He could die anyway, of exposure, while this madman carried on with his performance in the kitchen.

She tried again to divert his attention. 'The cop isn't my manfriend. I don't even know him, we just met.'

He shook his head, tutting. 'Girl. No-one games a gamer. I saw you two cooing at each other over the table. Our hero cop's going to be all torn up inside when he comes in and finds you all ... still.' He lingered over the word.

As he spoke, he walked around the table, and this time, when his fingers trailed over her neck, they stayed there.

She took a deep breath and held it, then took another. If he was going to choke her, she needed to give herself as much of a chance as she could. She'd scuba dived for years, even tried her hand at free diving. She knew how to oxygenate her lungs. But, as hard as she tried, she couldn't stop the moan of distress from erupting.

Her cool-headed analysis of how much air she could hold

evaporated. Science, facts, oxygen levels ... what did any of that matter now? He'd got what he wanted – she was beyond terrified. She was going to die, like her parents had. Like Aggie. Her lungs heaved wildly, her control broken.

He leaned his head down next to hers, so they were cheek to cheek. She could smell the sour stench of booze on his breath, feel a cold slug of saliva transfer itself from his wet lips.

'Like a doll,' he said, his voice returning to its sing-song cadence. His hands moved through her hair rhythmically, as though he were in a trance, and then his fingers firmed, their length forming a collar that tightened, and tightened, and tightened.

'Cry, little doll,' he sang into her neck. 'And your game will soon be over.'

Black spots were pooling in front of her eyes, and her throat and chest were bursting with the need to breathe. *I'll see you soon*, Aggie, she thought. *I'll be with you soon.* An image of her dear grandmother slid over her vision, tutting and crossing her arms, and saying *nuh-uh. No way. It's too soon, Lisa my lamb.*

But then Aggie's image evaporated and was replaced by a shadow of a man. No! Not a shadow, but a reflection! Ryan's reflection loomed in the window across the table from her – with an axe raised high over his head and an oath ripping loud from his mouth – and then her eyes went dark and her lungs ceased their struggle and she slid quietly into the black.

***

Later, much later, the serial killer Elliott Fox had been driven down the road in the custody of the Dunstone Sheriff's Department. The paramedics had pronounced Lisa bruised but okay, and stitched sixteen loops of synthetic gut through the gash in Ryan's head. Lisa lay sprawled across the sofa before the fire nursing a hot cocoa while Ryan filled her in.

He prodded the logs in the fire, turning them so their white-hot undersides broke into new flame. She'd slept – long and deeply – after the paramedics left, buffered from her thoughts by the sedative they'd given her. The pale fingers of early morning sun had woken her, and she'd come downstairs to find Ryan keeping watch while she recovered.

'We can thank Mister Darcy, really,' he said, stooping to give the old boy a pat. The dog was sporting his own line of stitches from ear to ear, like a spiky caterpillar crawling over the shaved patch of his head. 'When I went outside, he cleared off into the bushes. Fox had strung a trip wire out from the woodshed to a tree, and when I fell over it, he must have clouted me over the head. I was out cold, but not for long, I think. The dog must have attacked him, and got his head whacked too.'

Lisa took a sip of her drink, letting the hot milk soothe her ragged throat. 'I heard him bark, then yelp. That's when I started worrying. Then when that monster came in carrying the dog's collar and your gun ... I thought the worst.'

Ryan came over to the couch and sat next to her, hauling her up against him. She settled into the warmth, wondering at how right it felt. The drama of their ordeal had drawn them closer. Two strangers, one no longer feeling quite so lonely and grief-stricken, and the other? She hoped Ryan felt as good about being drawn together as she did.

'The dog must have recovered before me and set off for the vet's place,' he continued. 'Somehow, he managed to convince Toby that all hell had broken loose up here at the cabin, because Toby got into his four-wheel drive and came haring up here to see why Mister Darcy had his head ripped open. He brought his rifle, thinking there might be a bear up here. He drove into the yard just as I was making sure Fox was tied up.'

'Toby,' she smiled. 'He's a good guy.'

She felt Ryan huff out a laugh. 'Took him a while to figure out I was one of the good guys, though. I had to do a bit of quick talking while he pointed his shotgun at my guts. You were unconscious still tied to the table, I was tying up a guy and wielding an axe and had blood running down my face. It was quite a moment, I can tell you. Luckily, he kept a cool head, and helped me get you onto the couch. He had a CB radio in his truck so called the local cops.'

She reached out a hand to place her mug on the side table, then turned so she was facing Ryan. 'What a day, huh?'

He smiled, in a lopsided way that tugged at her heart. His hair was all over the place, and he had deep shadows beneath his eyes.

She held her hand to his cheek. 'Thank you for saving me.'

He brought his hand up and held hers. 'Fox was my problem. He followed me here. You'd never have been in danger if I hadn't bought your grandmother's cabin.'

She said the words that were in her heart. 'If that was the price I had to pay to meet you, I'd pay it twice over.'

He pressed a ghost of a kiss on her lips. 'Me too.'

She lay curled in the crook of Ryan's arm, her feet resting on the lump of fur that was Mister Darcy, snoozing noisily before the fire.

'We'll find some other way to get around the will,' Ryan said. 'This is California. People challenge wills all the time. Court cases are as popular as baseball and divorce.'

'The words were pretty clear. Unless I can find the new will, Aggie's estate is all sold off, and the proceeds go to charity as she has no "natural living issue". I'm adopted.'

'It's crazy. Such an old-fashioned definition of family.'

'Dunstone is an old-fashioned town. Jarrod Withers Senior probably used some template drawn up a century ago.'

She felt his hand run through her hair, linger gently over the still sore muscles of her neck.

'I've been hoping you'll stay anyway, even if we can't make the title over to you,' he said. 'So we can see where all this … between you and me … is going.'

She grinned and twisted her face upwards to plant a kiss on his mouth. 'I've been hoping you'd ask me.'

He left his lips on hers when she would have turned away, and the kiss she'd intended as thanks turned into something with a lot more smolder and intent.

'How's the neck?' he muttered, as his hands ran ribbons of fire up her sides.

'How's the headwound?' she countered, pulling his shirt out from his belt so she could slide a hand up over that warm, warm skin.

He groaned, and hauled her up on his knee, but just as she was about to slide into the heat of his embrace, her eyes focused on a shaft of sunlight sending dust motes dancing above a book wedged into the corner of a book shelf. 'Hang on a second. Oh, of course, of course!'

'Of course what? What is it?'

She grabbed Ryan's face between her hands. 'Mister Darcy. He was the clue all along.'

He frowned. 'I'm not following.'

Lisa jumped off his knee and went to the book shelf, pulling an old red hardback from the shelf. 'You know what this is?'

He grinned. '*Pride and Prejudice*?'

She grinned back at him. 'You're not just a handsome face

and a good kisser, Detective Mulligan.'

'So all the girls say.'

She hurried over and returned to the warm spot next to him on the sofa.

'You ready?' he said.

In answer, she opened the thin board of the cover. Nestled inside was onion-thin paper, neatly folded in three. Her fingers shook as she opened it and began to read the handwritten words. *This is the last will and testament of me, Agatha Wendall, of River's End Road. I hereby revoke all previous wills ...*

She looked up, tears of joy brimming over. 'Oh Ryan. I really am home.'

THE END

Turn the page to read an extract from Stella Quinn's contemporary romance novel *Tropic Storm*.

STELLA QUINN

EXTRACT FROM *TROPIC STORM*

Charlotte Jones paused amid the crowded departure lounge of Los Angeles International Airport. Shining up at her from the display rack at the front of an airport shop was the familiar cover of Bella magazine. But was it the latest issue?

She broke into a grin as she pulled the glossy magazine out of its stand. Her last article had made the cover, she hadn't expected that. A dancer slumped on a backstage prop, all heels and legs and bling, her oversize feathers discarded on the floor beside her. Charlotte ran a finger over the dancer's weary face, the loud pop of color from the flamingo pink of the feather. The photographer had nailed it this time.

'You buying that, lady? You wanna library, you're gonna have to go someplace else.'

'Relax, I'm buying,' she said, and placed the magazine down on the counter. She'd have a copy waiting for her when she returned home to London, stuffed into her front door mail slot, wrapped in a yard of bio-degradable plastic, but why wait? She'd never got over the thrill of seeing her freelance articles in print. Besides, she had a six hour flight ahead of her. She'd be able to read the magazine cover to cover.

'A bottle of water too, thanks.'

She rifled through the pound notes in her purse until she found her clip of American money, then handed a ten dollar note to the rumpled man at the till. Leaving the change on the counter, she headed back into the flow of people moving about the vast airport and cast a look upward to the overhead screens. The letters clicked over on a departure board, white font over a black background: Hawaiian Airlines to Honolulu, terminal 5, gate 58.

She felt a quiver of anticipation. This was a holiday she needed. Badly. And in a few hours more, it would begin. As much as she loved her job writing opinion pieces in women's magazines, and her hobby-slash-obsession writing for her blog, she needed some time to recover before going on assignment again. Two glorious weeks of time. She closed her eyes, and imagined the sunshine, salt water and sea breezes soothing her jangled nerves.

The queue to enter the waiting lounge at her gate was already snaking down the corridor by the time she made her way through the sprawling airport. Couples leaned on each other, taking selfies to pass the time; children squealed and bounced with excitement; an elderly woman wearing pearls the size of mothballs was having a heated discussion with a check-in attendant about the size of her carry-on luggage.

Charlotte smiled. People, chatter, hustle-and-bustle: she'd forgotten how much she used to enjoy the chaos of travel. And today, despite the crowds, she felt good. She felt strong, for the first time in months. Perhaps her psychologist was right, and time would heal her post-traumatic stress.

A tinny voice from overhead broke her train of thought. Just as well – now was not the time to be dwelling on what had happened to her in Barwick three months ago. *Passengers on flight HA4 to Honolulu, your plane has been delayed. Please remain near the departure gate and await further instruction.*

A collective groan issued from the people queued about her. She sighed, and shuffled forward as the family ahead of her went through the security check. She'd spent a lot of time in airport lounges over the years. What was an hour or two more?

She slung her leather carry-all on to the conveyor belt, showed her passport and ticket to the check-in attendant and was waved through to the dubious comfort of the holding area. At least there were seats available. She chose a plastic chair by the window, and settled in to wait, rolling her shoulders to relax some of the kinks. It had been a long flight over from London, and she was tired.

She read her article to pass the time. Bella Magazine had been her first serious job, back when she'd thought being an investigative reporter in war torn countries would be a great way to prove to the world that she had made something of herself that counted. She'd learned so much there, honed her craft, but eventually realized her skills lay in a different direction.

Luckily for her, she'd been to school for a time with the magazine's news editor. Antonia still contracted her for the odd article, which helped keep the funds flowing in. And this one had been a delight to write. It wasn't her usual piece – she was more at home advising women on ways to hop, skip and jump over the gender pay gap, or reviewing the latest mindfulness apps bombarding the market – but something about the chorus girls in London's latest stage show had appealed to her. The hard graft behind the glamour, the sweat beneath the sequins: she had found something when she interviewed the dancers which had resonated with her. The drive to succeed came at a price. For the dancers, it was the injuries, the uncertainty of work ahead, the competition for work within a shrinking industry.

Charlotte knew about paying a price for success. She'd spent the last decade paying it. In the early years of her career travel had kept her alone, often dangerous travel, reporting from remote locations via satellite phone, pursuing stories and leads in the dangerous alleyways of the world's cities. Since she'd gone freelance and started her blog, *Finding Happy*, she'd had so little time. To succeed in her career, she'd needed to put relationships second, herself second. The articles, the blog posts: she'd made them her number one priority. At least, she had until Barwick, when writing a blog post had landed her in hospital with a broken rib and a fractured arm and an unpredictable problem with panic.

A boarding announcement sounded from the overhead speakers, breaking her train of thought. Flashing a look over to the departure screen to check the time, her gaze fell on a dark-suited figure entering the lounge and all thoughts of Barwick fled from her brain.

'Oh, my,' she breathed.

Her jet-lagged muscles were instantly forgotten, as was the discomfort of her plastic chair. A handsome man was walking through the security screening area. She studied him covertly over her magazine. Six foot one, she decided, skimming the length of him from his close cropped, dark blond hair to his expensively shod feet. His suit was the darkest grey, emphasizing the white of his collar and cuffs, and the body it covered left Charlotte's lips forming an oh of admiration. She wondered what color his eyes were, and glanced up at his face only to encounter him looking back at her with shocked recognition.

She dropped her eyes to the magazine she held in her hand,

and felt blood rushing up to her throat and heating her cheeks.

Jack.

The calm she had been feeling, the happy puff of anticipation about starting her holiday, evaporated. She gazed blindly at her hands, gripping the *Bella* issue as though it was a lifeline, overwhelmed by a sudden riot of emotion. Why did it have to be Jack?

She peeled her fingers off the magazine, noting how clammy her palms had become. She had to calm the hell down. Finding herself in the same departure lounge as the man who had smashed her world to smithereens nine years ago ... it was too, too much. Maybe she could have dealt with it calmly if she wasn't already a mess about the fiasco in Barwick. But the fiasco had happened, and she was all out of bravery.

She kept her eyes averted, knowing she was behaving like a big chicken, but unable to help herself. Hopefully he'd have the decency to stay well away from her; she did not know if she could handle a confrontation with the man she had once been foolish enough to lose her heart to.

It was with relief some minutes later that Charlotte heard the boarding call for her flight. The airline companies fit three hundred people on these planes – with luck, they'd be seated well away from each other. She had an eye mask in her bag, ear plugs. She'd wrap an airline blanket around her head if she had to. She could not face Jack. Not now, not ever.

She slung her bag over her shoulder, checking her belongings were all safely tucked away, then rose to her feet. She marched swiftly over to the boarding gate, checked her pass, then took off down the long airbridge to the plane. It wasn't until she'd sunk into the plush comfort of her seat that she relaxed and closed her eyes. She was safe.

Her phone buzzed, and she reached to silence it. The words

Antonia is calling scrolled over the glass screen. She sighed. Antonia wasn't just the editor of Bella magazine – she'd have ended the call if she was. Antonia was also one of her oldest friends, and was not the sort of person you could ignore, even from half a world away.

She lifted the phone to her ear, and braced herself for the onslaught.

'Charlotte, have you arrived? Tell me everything. Is the water warm? Are the cocktails cold? Wait. Any single guys? You know I've got weeks of holiday owing, I can be there like a shot if there's single guys.'

Nothing changed. She smiled. 'Toni, I'm nowhere near Hawaii. I'm parked on a tarmac in the States. No cocktail umbrellas in sight.'

'Bummer. Call me the instant you get to the hotel, won't you? I'll worry if you don't.'

'Yes, matron.'

'None of that cheek from you, young lady. But seriously, how are you coping with the crowds. No dramas in the airports?'

She closed her eyes, and a vision of the grey-suited drama called Jack came into view. 'Not that sort of drama, no.'

There was a pause. Charlotte imagined her friend's brain scrambling through the innuendo of that remark. She chuckled to herself at Toni's next words.

'Tell. Me. Everything.'

She let out a breath. Was she ready to talk about it? She sighed, and took the plunge. 'You'll never guess the man I just saw at LAX.'

'Umm. A Hemsworth? Hugh Grant? Colin Firth?'

'Somebody I actually know.'

There was a pause. 'I'm struggling here, Charlotte. You live like a nun. Do you even know any men? I can't think of a single one you've given tuppence about since Jack bloody Diamond back when you were a cadet journalist in London and I was backpacking my way through the single men of Europe.'

The silence stretched out as Charlotte waited for the penny to drop. Or tuppence, in this case.

'You're not seriously telling me you ran into Jack Diamond?'

'Yep. The rat himself.'

'I'm speechless.'

Charlotte laughed. 'Well that's a first.'

'So, what happened?'

'I ran away.'

'Ran away? You? Charlotte the bad-ass women-are-champions blogging queen?'

She could hardly believe it herself. But the heart was a tender thing, and she'd forgotten how tender hers could feel. 'It was actually pretty tough seeing him, Toni.'

She could hear her friend's nails tapping on a hard surface. Antonia was at work, no doubt, ripping adverbs out of some hapless reporter's article.

'Yeah, I bet,' Toni said at last. 'Listen, Charlotte, I have to take a call from Barcelona, but we should talk this out. Oh, and you know that draft article you gave me? The one on the Barwick riots?'

Oh yeah, she knew that one alright. She'd written it up in her hospital bed, well, dictated it into her phone, as her arm had been buried within six inches of plaster. Thousands of words on the hapless blogger who'd been on her way to a café to interview a woman about a community gardening project, but instead found herself in the middle of a riot that swept through the regional city when police shot a man in the street. She almost regretted having written it now – she'd been too raw, too deeply affected to be objective in her reporting. Antonia could bin it, that was fine. 'Don't worry about the article, I shouldn't have sent it in.'

'Don't worry about it? Girlfriend, it is fantastic. I've entered it into the press awards. It's taking center stage in the next issue of Bella.'

'Antonia—' She drifted to a close. Thinking about that day still had the power to upset her. She'd not be reading the article when it was published.

She heard her friend sigh down her end of the phone. 'Charlotte. We don't have to talk about this now, forget I mentioned it, okay? Why don't you skype me when you're settled in Hawaii, okay? I'll invite Sabrina over to my place, and the three of us can bitch about men and bossy editors until you get that sad little sound out of your voice. I don't like hearing it.'

Charlotte smiled. Bossy or not, Antonia was as fabulous as a friend could be. 'It's a date. And thanks.'

She slipped her phone over into airplane mode and dropped it into her bag. She was lucky to have Antonia and Sabrina in her life, and she knew it. Her old school chums had been there for her through thick and thin.

The muted hubbub of the filling plane was comfortingly familiar. She turned to her window, and gazed across the vacant seat through to the busy airstrip. Only a few more hours until her holiday started. The website for the holiday accommodation she was travelling to had displayed a gallery of glorious photographs. Part of the Jewel Resort Group, the Jewel of Oahu promised self-contained villas set amid lush Hawaiian gardens, with views spanning a perfect private beach and the Pacific Ocean beyond.

She sank into an indulgent daydream of bathing in sun-dappled water, and lying in the feathered shade of coconut palms. She could think about the project her psychologist had been encouraging her to pursue, or maybe read the half-dozen books she had included in her luggage. She smiled. Would she read the romcom first? Or the new thriller that—

'Excuse me.'

Charlotte opened her eyes and sat up abruptly, reaching out an instinctive hand to smooth down her wayward auburn hair. Oh no. Fate couldn't be so cruel.

Dear Reader

I hope you are enjoying my stories. To keep in touch, come check out my website and sign up to the newsletter so I can let you know when I have a new release.
Happy reading!

Stella Quinn

ABOUT THE AUTHOR

Stella Quinn believes romance, adventure and escape are the reasons we love to read.

Her **Holiday Romance Novel** series includes *Tropic Storm*, *Stowaway* and *Island Fling*. These novels are sun-filled and sea-drenched; love blooms under the palm trees of far-flung islands, or in the warm waters above sunken wrecks. *Tropic Storm* was long-listed for the RWA Emerald Award in 2017, *Stowaway* came 2nd in the RWA Emerald Award in 2018, and *Island Fling* won the RWA Valerie Parv Award in 2018.

Her **Short & Sweet Romance** short stories are available as promotions and free reads from time to time. Titles include *Finding Betty-Lou*, a rural romance, *The Raven's Curse*, a Victorian romance, and *Beneath the Waves*, a contemporary romance that was a finalist in the RWA Little Gem Award in 2017 (and published in the anthology that year).

Her **A Stella Novella** series is underway, the first being the Christmas special *Catching Snow*.

What do readers think? Here are some reader comments: "wow", "captured me from the first page", "loved it", "loved the backstory", "everything worked!"